D1015916

SECRETS & LIES 4

By

H.M. WARD

LAREE BAILEY PRESS
www.HMWard.com

COPYRIGHT

LAREE BAILEY PRESS
First Edition: MAY 2016
ISBN: 9781630351229

SECRETS & LIES 4

CHAPTER 1

Carter stands there in faded black clothes, his pants two sizes too big. His dark hair is slicked away from his eyes, damp with sweat or rain. I can't tell which. His cheeks are rosy as if he's been running. My gaze drops to Carter's feet as I pull away from Nate. I wish we were standing closer to the door. If Carter had smacked it into us, there would have been confusion and a way to cover up the kiss. But this? There's no way it looks like anything else.

Carter won't fall for the 'oops, I fell on his lips' defense. He's intelligent, and I respect him despite our argument, so I don't make excuses. There are none. I tuck a strand of hair behind my ear and shift my weight to my other foot.

Nate swallows hard, caught between breaths as Carter walked in. The two of them freeze, looking at one another in horror. It feels like the longest twenty minutes of my life, but it couldn't have been more than a few seconds.

Resisting the urge to hang my head in shame, I glance up at Carter, who's sporting a sucker-punched expression. I manage to find my voice. Stepping toward him, I say casually, "Hey, Carter! I was just headed out. Come with me." It isn't a question. It's a demand—and based on the circumstances, it's a little insane.

When he stands there blinking, unable to close his gaping mouth or stop staring at Nate, I side step between them. He shakes his head and frowns, "Kerry, what the hell—"

Carter doesn't get a chance to finish. I sigh exasperated, as Nate remains paralyzed. This kiss will cost him his job. They'll say he was sexually harassing me or worse. I'm not going to let that happen. Right now I need Carter's feet moving down the hall.

I'm going to have to make something up. Fast. So I wing it. Grinning, I go up on the balls of my feet and press my lips to his. Carter blinks, shocked, but he doesn't pull away. A small spark shoots through me and flitters into my belly like a falling leaf.

I feel Nate's gaze on the side of my face and inwardly squirm. Maybe this was stupid. Okay, it was dumb. There's no way Carter is going to think I'm loose, throwing myself at anyone with a dick. Although, I suppose that's exactly what I've been doing. Nate's still glaring at us, not happy, but remaining mute.

Carter kisses me, or stands there stunned—it depends on how you look at it—with his hands at his sides. Heat rushes to his face, flushing it with embarrassment and although I expected shock, I thought he'd kiss me back. When he doesn't, I pull back.

Beaming up at him, I grab his hand and pull. "Come on. I have to get ready, and you're not dropping this class. I need you." I don't say anything else. I don't elaborate.

Nate is silent, rooted in place, with his brow furrowed and his hands at his sides. I get the distinct impression he has no one to talk to—at least, not about the crazy-ass bus girl that landed in his bed before he discovered she was his student. Nate seems isolated. That's probably what drew me to him in the first place, more so than the sketchpad. I felt utterly alone that night, and he was giving off the same vibe. Like calls to like.

I toss the thoughts to the back of my mind and tug Carter behind me while prattling about

Jax being an ass. "This whole stupid thing is a mess, and I can't back down. Actually," I pull Carter into the empty classroom and step past him to shut the door before flicking the lights on. I can't force my eyes off the floor even as my eyebrows inch into my hairline. My lips are parted, stuck in an unending sigh because I don't know what to say. I want things back the way they were.

I miss him.

Carter doesn't blink. He's still shocked, lost inside his mind. It's probably a museum for paintings of memories and sculptures of dreams. Carter seems like the kind of guy that files things away to pull out later. My brain is a typhoon of emotion. My favorite memories eroded the day Matt dumped me for Mom. I still have to deal with them this weekend. Can life fuck me any harder? I shouldn't ask that, but really? How can it get worse? The raccoon bites me, and I grow a third tit? That might be helpful. I make a mental note to hug the fuzzy bastard the next time I'm on the bus.

I press my back to the door and glance up at him. I'm worried about this—about him—and Nate. "Listen, I've screwed up this whole rebound thing beyond belief." I laugh nervously, lowering my head and letting my hair fall across my face. I tuck a long strand of bland brown hair behind my ear and talk to my sneakers. "Every guy I've thrown myself at has rejected me."

The best deceivers use the truth to twist a perfect lie. I'm not the most convincing liar, and I hate being dishonest, but it's not my job on the line. It's Nate's. And this wasn't his fault—it was mine. I can't let Carter tell the dean about it when I'm the one to blame, so that's what I'll do. I'll shift all the blame to myself. Flicking my gaze up at him, I laugh nervously.

He stands there in the open space, his hands shoved in his pockets and an indifferent expression on his face. Maybe I shouldn't say it. Maybe it's cruel. I don't know, and that's my biggest problem.

I press my lips together and feel my heart crack inside my chest. Words begin to spill out of my mouth, and once I start, I can't shut up. "Since I got here, my life has turned into a clusterfuck of epic proportions. I've made one wrong move after another, and it won't stop. I can't undo this. I wish I could."

Without looking at me, Carter finally says something. "What part would you erase? Losing your friends? Strutting around naked? Hooking up with the professor? Or kissing me?" His eyes are resentful and hot on the side of my face.

Something inside me snaps. That's it. He can't treat me like a slut for modeling. He's part of the same world, and there are rules. He knows that as damned well as I do. I step toward him, place both hands on his chest, and shove. "Hey! I don't deserve your scorn or your anger. We're artists, you and me. We were on the same page at one point. You know as well as I do that modeling isn't the same as stripping or prostitution, so stop being such an asshole! As if things aren't hard enough, I don't need you dropping your conflicted morality crap on me right now. You think you're the only one who doesn't like Beth's brother hanging around? Well, neither do I! I can't get rid of him, believe me, I've tried."

Carter's face crinkles and I know he's getting mad. He snaps, "Yeah, well you didn't try hard enough."

I make an aggravated sound in the back of my throat that's lost somewhere between a scream and a growl. My arms tense and my fingers splay at my sides. I start talking with my hands, extremely aware of how close I am to poking my eyes out waving my five digits around wildly. "You have no fucking clue how hard I've tried! Since day one, the first second, before I even got to class my life started falling apart. I've done everything I could do to pull myself back together again. I thought you were my friend." My voice changes abruptly, and I can't hide my disgust. "We aren't supposed to look at a nude model and think sex. It's shadow and light, curves and lines—it's a moment to be captured and immortalized."

"I know that!" He's angry now, stepping back as he tries to keep his temper in check.

I get in his space and yell up into his face, "Then why are you giving me such a hard time? Why does it matter what I do? You've known me for five minutes. You have no idea what's going on in my life!"

"Kerry—"

"You have friends here. You know how everything works—from Jax's tricks, to Beth's idiotic brothers—and I don't."

"Kerry, wait—"

"I'm still figuring out where the cafeteria is and how the hell I'm supposed to deal with my mom fucking my boyfriend! Carter, I'm living in a shitstorm with no one to help me, and the one person I should be able to depend on for anything—well, it turns out she's the reason my soul mate left me in the first place." There are tears in my eyes. I wipe them away angrily, stomp across the room, and sit on a table.

I've said everything I wanted to say. The storm raging inside of me is spent, and I feel tired and melancholy. Carter remains across the room, still poised by the door.

When he finally starts to say something, I cut him off. I don't want to have the rest of this conversation right now. "Don't tell the dean. I can't handle it right now, and it was my fault. I did it. There was nothing out of line from Professor Smith." Lifting my gaze, I look to Carter hoping he'll agree.

When he doesn't answer, anger seeps back into my veins. Fine, judge me. I shake my head in disgust. "Listen, class starts in five minutes. We don't have time for this. I made a mistake. He just stood there shocked, same as you."

Carter remains where he is, across the room, a stone's throw away. "I didn't hear anything. I was there to drop this class. I can't deal with you—"

"Gee, thanks."

His voice softens. "That's not what I meant. Let me finish. I can't deal with seeing you naked up there. It's my problem, not yours. I shouldn't have taken it out on you. It just threw me off." He runs his hand over his head and down his neck, lets out a sigh, and stares at me. "It's supposed to be what you said—there shouldn't be anything more—but I don't feel like that around you."

"Could have fooled me," I say. "I kissed you. Remember? For all practical purposes, I could have been a softball, and you would have reacted the same way."

"You're not a softball." His voice is a whisper.

"Right, I'm a nut ball who tried to start a three-way with my teacher and another student."

He chokes, covering his lips with his hand to hide a smile. "Kerry, it wasn't that bad."

I'm sitting on the edge of the table, leaning forward with my hands at my hips, and my elbows locked. I'm swinging my feet and shaking my head, trying to avoid his gaze. "Yes, it was. I was there, remember? I might as well have written ménage à trois on his desk with an Expo marker."

As I say the last word, something happens and my center of gravity inadvertently moves forward. My big head is already leaning pretty far forward, and that tiny movement puts it past my knees. Next thing I know I'm face-planting on the linoleum.

Carter rushes forward. "Are you all right? Damn, Kerry!" His hand is on my arm.

I'm spread-eagle, with my face against the cold floor. I roll over slowly, too embarrassed to move any faster. I stare up at him and want to cry. "This summarizes my life. Threatening to topple at the least imbalance and any flashes of happiness are fleeting—I always end up flat on my face."

"I didn't need a demonstration." He grins and holds out his hand. "Use your words, Kerry." He says it in the same voice a parent would use with a toddler.

It makes me laugh a little. I put my hand in his palm. He pulls me up, and I'm standing in front of him, with his hand in mine. "Life sucks. I want a do-over."

"Yeah, I get that. Believe me. I understand the whole life blows thing, but there are no do-overs. You have to make the most of whatever hand you got dealt this round. Next time will be better."

"You haven't known me long enough. Next round is going to catch on fire." I jab my free thumb into my chest. "I'm THAT girl."

Carter's expression is soft and kind. He watches me for a moment, his eyes moving along the curve of my cheek and then dropping to our hands. "I'm not okay sitting in this class and drawing you. I can't be detached."

"So don't be. Be attached. Be a fucking emotionally available hard-on American male. Carter, maybe it'll take you in a direction as an artist that you haven't imagined."

"Yeah." He swallows hard. "That's why I'm worried. I don't want to be a rebound, Kerry." He lifts my hand to his lips and places a soft kiss on my skin.

It's so sweet I can't help it—I smile. "I'm going to be emotionally unavailable for a while. That was the PC way of saying I'm going batshit crazy and plan to focus pretty fucking hard on the crazy for a while. I feel like I don't know who I am." My brows knit together and I find myself trying to catch his eye, wishing I had his approval.

"So find out. When you do, I'll still be here." He offers a half smile and drops my hand. That surprises me. It seems as if his anger has faded and he's ready to put everything behind us and move forward.

"What about Professor Smith? And the class?"

"I don't know what you're talking about with Smith. I wasn't in his office tonight." He winks at me, and a lazy smile spreads across his lips. "If you don't mind me being here—"

"I want you here."

"Then I'll stay in the class."

CHAPTER 2

Holy Hell, that was insane. Carter seems appeased for the moment, and what he wants is out there in the open. At one time, such an honest declaration of intentions would have made my panties drop to my ankles in a lead-like thump. But now? Not so much.

I don't know what's wrong with me. Maybe I have supersized PMS, and I won't feel better until I scream my head off and punch something. I kick off my sweats and get naked behind the makeshift screen (which is actually a hugeass supply cabinet) in the back of the classroom. Carter is waiting in his seat, and the door is open.

I hear Nate pad into the room. He clears his throat and speaks softly. I peak around the corner of the cabinet and see Nate and Carter talking. I get the impression they know each other—like beyond the classroom. It's just a sense, and there's no evidence to support it. I pause, listening. Too bad I can't hear anything.

I call out, "I need the drape."

Nate turns, and, when his eyes sweep over my face, I know there are more words there—things unsaid, regret, and something more. He nods, no longer urging me to quit. Crossing the room, he opens one of the many cabinets lining the far wall and pulls out the same drape as last week. He carries it across the open space and hands it to me. "Here."

I take it with both hands and wrap the fabric over my shoulders, before stepping out into the room. I probably shouldn't ask him for help, but it's either taunt Carter with my nakedness or ask the man who's already seen my ass to help me cover it.

"You're frowning. What's wrong?" Nate asks softly. His hair falls over his forehead as his gaze sweeps the set he recreated from last time. He must have set it up before Carter and I arrived tonight. Nate steps forward, moves the chaise slightly, then steps back.

"I need help with the drape."

He stops tipping his head at the little set and glances at me. "Right, of course. Please sit and I'll move it into position."

This moment is the definition of awkward. Carter is watching us intently while Nate tries not to touch me at all. It's like I'm carrying a pox, and he's afraid he'll catch it. Stop thinking. This is shadows and light. He isn't thinking about anything else—like parting my thighs and lying on top of me. The memory of Nate's strong hands on my hips flashes through my mind and fades like a shooting star. Move on, Kerry. That part of your screwed up life is gone.

At least I think it is, but the way Nate is looking at me right now, coupled with that kiss in his office has me wondering if he changed his mind. Maybe he wants a fuckbuddy after all? The thing about one-nighters and me—I kind of wish they lasted longer than one night.

I carefully arrange myself on the chaise and adjust the drape so that it still covers me as I slide down sideways onto my hip. When I position my arms to their previous placement, the drape drops and pools at my hips. There's a little side-boob showing, but nothing else.

Nate grabs the edge and pulls. The fabric slips away, chilling me as it goes.

"Kerry," Carter calls out, "your legs are in the wrong position. Last time, the top one was extended."

"Right." I feel the blush on my cheeks and am glad I'm facing in the other direction. I shift my legs and inadvertently pull the fabric as I move.

Nate moves back to the foot of the chaise, and rearranges the material, pooling the fabric into a waterfall of folds.

"Sorry."

Nate glances up at me, and I can tell he wants to say something, but he doesn't. Instead, he tweaks the rest of the set and adjusts the lights.

Students begin filing in and grabbing their sketches from last time. Emily walks by without a word. I think she's still pissed at me. I consider jumping up and giving her a big bear hug, but I think that would make things worse.

With all the students settled, Nate starts teaching like he did last week. He stands in front of me, but I can still see him out of the corner of my eye.

Nate explains, "The S-curve in this pose is important. See the way her back, hips, and shoulders curve almost like the letter S? When choosing a pose, this curve is fundamental. The easiest way to arrange the pose is to have the model put all her weight on one leg. It naturally throws out the hip helping define that curve. In this case, our model is seated. It would be very easy to make her waist appear blockish. To avoid that, she has one knee pulled up—" he points to the pad of my foot that's poking out from under the knee of my top leg, "and the other leg extended. It tilts her hips in the right direction so that when she places an arm on the back of the chaise and pivots at the waist to look at her feet—Miss Hill, would you be so kind?"

I do as he asks and stare at my toes. My lashes are lowered and my expression pensive. I've often wondered what models think about while posing. If they are excited to be in front of people or worried about looking fat? Now that I'm up here, I can tell you—we think about everything.

Did I turn off the iron?

Chelsey is a jerk. I need to do something with that.

Pringles sound really good. I'm going to eat an entire can for dinner.

I'll have to walk to the quad to get it.

I'm sick of letting people walk all over me.

That leads my thoughts to Mom. How am I supposed to be okay with her and Matt when it's clearly not okay? She gave birth to me. I should get over it. At the same time, she could give birth to a sibling and then Matt could be my stepdad. Fuck that. I'm not on board.

How do I live with her stupid decision? I want to tell her to screw off. I don't want to live with it. Every time the thought roams through my mind, I want to shoot it. It doesn't belong there. Your mom isn't supposed to nail your boyfriend. Some things are off limits. At least I thought they were.

It's something about sitting without anything to look at or read—no TV, no book—that makes your mind wander and churn up the muck plaguing you. Models have to be completely insane to want to do this long-term—or completely at peace with their lives and without problems.

I wish my life were simpler.

I've wished it so many times over the years. At some point, I had to accept that some people don't live peaceful lives. Shit falls from the sky, and they're the folks in the wrong place at the wrong time.

They're my people.

Nathan's voice has a soothing richness to it. I could listen to him all day. His paintings are different. They are raw and vibrant, sublime and searching. They boast a feeling of infinity and a clashing finality too powerful to contain.

If he painted me would the piece have the same movement and elegant brush strokes? Would I be beautiful or would he portray me as turbulently as the rest of his work?

The room falls silent, and I glance up. Nate is in his spot at the back, carefully avoiding looking in my direction. Not moving for hours is harder than you'd think. Every few seconds a finger wants to twitch or my leg wants to stretch.

I channel my thoughts elsewhere, but they keep swinging back to Matt. We were a couple for so long I forgot what it felt like to be alone. I saw him every day, gave him everything, did anything he wanted, and he still left me. I don't understand. We were happy—at least I thought we were. He'd tell me I was his 'baby girl,' and kiss my temple. When we were together, every kiss was slow and perfect. His mouth on my body was bliss. He loved me. There's no way he could be with me like that if he didn't, right? I mean, I should have known. I would have seen it.

But I didn't. The truth didn't materialize until I was gone. I thought Matt and I were forever. Beth is right. I need a rebound guy. I need to figure out who I am and what I like. Maybe I don't want sweet, vanilla sex. We never did anything else. It didn't get carnal. There was always control and no one crossed the line. Hell, neither of us even had the line on the horizon. Besides the initial discovery of where stuff was and what it looked like, we did the deed the old fashioned way—the thingy went in the traditional hole. I'd been okay with that. I guess Matt wasn't. Maybe he wanted to do something he couldn't ask me to do, so he asked—

Oh, God! That's a horrifying thought—I'm the prude, and my mother's the slut, so he asked her.

I don't want to win him back. I just want to stop mourning over something that turned out to be worthless.

*****

The class ends without incident. Everyone packs up their things and leaves.

As I dress behind the cabinet, I wonder if karma is real. If it is, what the hell did I do to deserve this? I tug on my sweats and pull my hair into a ponytail before walking out into the room. It's so quiet I thought I was alone, but, as I turn around the screen, I see Emily sitting there, waiting for me.

She's got her blue hair poofed high on her head and a matching blue hoop earring in her nose. The black collar around her neck is spiked and partially hidden by the black leather duster covering her skintight black dress. "Hey."

"Hey," I echo back. "Are you here to kick my ass or invite me to go clubbing? And by clubbing, I mean maces—me and you—at the bitchy Barbie rush tonight." I smirk, not expecting it to be either. She's here to chew me out for modeling, for breaking Carter's heart, and, most heinously, for stealing her man. I'd have issues with that too. But I didn't know her first. I knew Carter. And I'm not her mother, so I don't owe her anything. I frown and slap my bag down on a desk, digging through it to find my wallet, and hoping I have enough cash to score a can of chips. Yeah, I'm still on that.

Pringles. The dinner of champions.

Emily snorts and folds her arms over her chest. "That would be amazing, but since the school frowns on bludgeoning sorority girls, I thought I'd make a peace offering."

And that's a weird turn of events. I stop pawing through my things and look up at her. "What'd you have in mind?"

"There's a haunted bar down on 6th Street. Come with? My treat." She offers a half-smile which is notable considering I didn't think her mouth could even move that way. She's usually sporting an expression so intense most people stop, turn around, and walk the other way. Emily has a severe case of RBF—resting bitch face— but she owns it, so it's all good.

"Really? So, what made you change your mind? I thought I was an insidious slut trying to poach your man? Why the sudden change of heart?" I realize I'm kicking a hornet's nest, but I need to know.

She blanches and steps toward me, trying to shake it off. "You offered to hook up with him, and he shot you down. That's good enough for me."

We're standing eye-to-eye. She's wearing purple contacts and blinks at me. I wonder if I should correct her, explain how Carter blew me off because he wants something real, not a one-night stand.

"How'd you know about that?" My stomach twists. We were in Nate's office. Did she see the whole thing?

She shrugs. "I was passing by and saw your embarrassing attempt at PDA. You were hot. He was cold. All is good with Emily again." She smiles brightly, which just looks wrong on her edgy, punk face.

So should I smooth things over with Emily or go home? I don't really want to go home. Bitchy Pants will be there now, and tomorrow my mom is coming with my ex in tow. I want to get sloshed and take my aggressions out on someone hot. I want to lose it and not care about what happens next.

I'm nodding and pulling my bag onto my shoulder, zipping the top as I say, "Sounds good. I'm in."

"Awesome. And to prove it to you, we are going to find you a rebound guy. Tonight. I'm not leaving until you've got a man to take home."

"And fuck senseless," I add hastily. At that moment, I glance up and see Nate in the doorway.

He waves a white envelope. "Your check, Miss Hill."

He heard me. I know he did. His eyes lock with mine and, for a brief second, the hairs on the back of my neck stand up. I'm thinking so loudly it's a scream in my mind.

I WANTED IT TO BE YOU! You said no. You rejected me. I wanted it to be you.

He holds out the check, and I reach for it. I can't help it. I mutter, "I'm crazy."

His blue gaze drops, and when he looks up again, he smiles. "I know. I like that about you."

A frown shadows my lips. As it spreads his gaze fixates on my mouth and I know there are things he wants to say, but he can't. Not here, not now. He clears his throat and nods. "Be careful ladies. There's been a lot of shit going on. I'd hate to see something happen to either of you."

Does he know I was drugged? He seems to be hinting at it. I didn't tell anyone. I'd rather they thought I screwed Josh than that I was stupid enough to get roofied.

Emily snorts and acts tough. "They already tried to get me, and this one here—she saved my ass." She throws her arm over my shoulder and tugs me close.

"Really?" Nate glances at me.

"Yeah. She was a great friend, and I was a bit of a jealous bitch. I'm really sorry, Kerry." Her moment of sincerity is short-lived. "Now, let's get shitfaced and find us a couple of fuckbuddies."

I laugh nervously and wish I were dead. Out of all people to say that to, why'd it have to be him? Emily walks out the door and marches down the hall, assuming I'm right behind her. "Come on, freshman!"

I linger for a second, wanting to tell him things, but unable to find words.

Nate's dark lashes lower as his gaze cuts to the side. His lips part once, then twice, before he says, "Goodnight."

"Right." What else can I say? I step toward the door at the same time he does so that we cross the threshold at the same time. We're pushed close together in the narrow space, and I do everything possible to avoid touching him, but at the last moment, when I move to turn away, I catch his shoulder. Our arms collide and for a brief moment, I feel his fingers brush against mine.

I glance up. "Sorry. I didn't mean to…"

I didn't mean to start things with you that can't be finished.

I didn't mean to put you in a weird spot.

I didn't mean to promise you friendship and have to hide it from everyone.

In that moment, I don't know what he is to me, and I can't hide my frustration much longer.

"Kerry," he breathes my name as our fingers intertwine. But then he steps away, and it's like it never happened.

"Come on, Kerry! Let's haunt the bar!" Emily laughs as she spins around to look back at us. "That was punny, right?"

I smile and tuck my chin as I walk away from Nate. Regret is trying to strangle me, but some things just aren't meant to be. Nate and I will never happen.

"Hilarious." I turn back to Nate for the last time. I say, "Goodnight," but it's clearly goodbye.

He could stop me. He could say he's interested and wants me for himself. But that doesn't happen. Emily is dancing at the end of the hall and calling out for me to join her. As I rush away, I feel his eyes on my back.

Nate watches us disappear down the stairwell without another word.

CHAPTER 3

The haunted bar was built in 1886 and apparently the owner suffered a bit of misfortune—as did every successive owner of this particular establishment. Whether they were shot, drowned, lost to flu, dragged by a horse, on even took a header down the stairs—regardless of age, race or wealth, they all mysteriously expired.

Emily is laughing. "It's as if the place were cursed. Sometimes the lights flicker, and they claim it's Jeb, the guy that croaked tumbling down the steps over there."

She points across the small room. We're sitting at a highly polished wooden bar, on stools covered in leather matching the hides displayed on the walls. PETA would hate this place. The ceiling is punched copper with a rustic design. There are too many horns and antlers on the walls for my taste, but this is Texas. There are a few seating areas behind us, small tables with copper brads and thick couches with tufted leather backs and big, comfy-looking armrests. The lighting is dim, and the bulbs are the warm, flickering kind reminiscent of gas lamps with real flames.

We both stare at the steps. They're smooth, long, and wide. I'm not feeling the danger. "Maybe he fell because it was dark and he haunts the place to keep the staircase safe and death-free."

Emily grins. "Or he's a mean bastard and is sick of being the only one to have an incident on those stairs. I mean look at them. How?" She leaves the word hanging in the air and blinks at the short staircase.

"Hey!" I point at her. "Don't be like that. People with bad luck can't help it. All sorts of shit happens to me. I must have been a total bitch in a past life."

Emily giggles and falls forward, pressing her head to the bar and then looking up at me. The dark makeup around her eyes is a little smeared. "You? Like Chelsey? Bacon! I mean, what the fuck is wrong with her? We need to send some bad mojo her way!"

"I'm working on it. If there's one thing you should remember about me, it's that I never forget a damned thing."

I'm looking down at the bottom of my third Long Island Iced Tea and wondering if I can do another. I skipped dinner and went straight for the booze. As it is, I have a pretty good buzz going on. Each drink has, what, four shots of alcohol? So that means I've had around— twelve—shots so far. Wait. That can't be right.

I frown. Okay, maybe I'm a little more than tipsy. I can't seem to do math, and the bar might be swaying a little bit. Fuck it. I lift my hand, and the bartender sees me and brings another drink. What the hell, right? I can still think and I'd rather not.

"You shouldn't take shit from anyone. Life's too short." Emily knocks back another shot of her weird black, tar-looking drink. She slaps it down hard on the wood. The little cup slips off the bar and falls, and then bounces off the wooden floor, before rolling onto the carpet.

"I got it." I jump up from my perch and follow the empty cup like a toddler trying to catch a butterfly. I don't think it's going to jump up and fly away, but I can't seem to convince my hands to drop. When I'm right above it, I accidentally kick the thing. "Fuck." It skitters across the room, bounces off a wall, and clunks down the stairs.

Emily starts laughing and waving a finger at me. "Do not go over there. You'll die, Kerry!" The giggles get the better of her, and she starts laughing into her arm.

"Oh, shut up, you—you." Great come back. I shake my head and plop my sneakers across the floor to the far side of the room and grab the railing. I'm about to head down the short flight of stairs when I feel a hand on my back.

"Kerry?"

That voice. I want to melt into him. I turn around, and Nate is there, dressed in the same outfit as earlier. His hair is messy, and his lips are swollen.

I blink at him. "Did you have sex? Wow, my voice is loud." I glance around looking for a reason why my voice fills the room. I half expect to find a floating bullhorn in front of my face, but there's nothing.

"Yes, it is."

I turn toward him--at least that was the plan. Now I'm leaning on him, and poking my finger into his stomach. "Well, Mr. Teacher, your lips are puffy. Did you finally get some?"

He smiles and looks back at the room and then at me. "My love life is not open for discussion at the moment."

"Mine is. Do you know why? Because there's nothing to tell." I frown and feel my bottom lip jut out. "I look like a crazy jock chick with my sweats and sneakers, and guys are afraid of Emily. At the rate things are going, I'm going to end up fucking her tonight."

Nate clears his throat and coughs into his hand. "Oh? I didn't know women interested you."

Still pouting, I explain, "They don't. Well, that's not entirely true. I like breasts."

He's grinning, still holding me up. "Who doesn't?"

I point at him like he understands me. "But I need more than that. Besides, I have my own. I want the scent of a guy on my body and everything from the sweat, to the fucking—I'm just not into girls. I'd be willing to make an exception to get over Matt, but, then he'd take credit for turning me gay, and tell people I totally lost my shit and swore off men after he dumped me."

Nate laughs. "I'm sorry, but if he's the only guy you've been with and you decided to hit for the other team because of him, that doesn't say he has much to offer the female half of the world."

My shoulders slump, and I'm ready to cry. "That's not what my mom said!"

"Is that a joke? Because I think you told it wrong." He cocks his head to the side and tries to see my face to tell if I'm serious, but I'm leaning against his chest.

Tears spring from my eyes and I shake my head. "No, it's not. I'm the joke. I can't do this, Nate. How am I supposed to look at them? How am I supposed to act like it doesn't matter when it does? They both stabbed me in the back, and they want me to be happy for them. I can't do it." I have a slight tug at the back of my mind. It's the voice of self-preservation telling me to shut the hell up, but I can't. Everything comes pouring out, and I keep thinking he already knows all of this stuff. Everyone else does.

"So don't." His hands are on my shoulders, steadying me. "Hey, calm down, Kerry. It'll be all right."

Tears and snot mix on my cheeks, and I know I look like a train wreck. "No, it won't. Don't you get it? They're coming here this weekend to see me and stay with me. I can't even think about it, never mind live it. There's only so much a person can take, and I'm bent so far past my breaking point I can literally kiss my own ass!" I'm crelling, that oh-so-sexy, snotified cry-yell of a crazy chick.

His hands squeeze my shoulders, and his voice is like a warm blanket. "Stay with me. Don't go home until they're gone."

Flabbergasted, I gape at him, jaw dragging on the carpet while trailing a line of shiny drool. "I'm sorry," I laugh and cry more, "but I'm hallucinating now. I'd also like to sleep with you and forget all this shit, but you kicked me to the curb more than once already. Can you hear me?" I wave my fingers in front of his face. I'm starting to think that fourth drink was a bad idea. Oh, God! My fingers are by his nose! I giggle through the tears and wiggle my fingertips.

Nate clasps his hand around my fingers, and I look up into his face. He's trying hard not to smile. "Yes, I can hear you. And I owe you one. You saved me that night."

I scoff and jerk my head back before jutting it forward again. If I had on hoop earrings, I'd have attitude all up in his face. "I did, and you've treated me like crap. I'm done with letting people treat me like I don't matter." My spine is straight, and my fingers are free from his hand, and one even had the audacity to flick his nose.

Nate swallows hard. "So your plan here tonight is to go home with Emily, then roll out the welcome mat for your mother and your ex with a nasty hangover?"

I sneer at him. "I don't do girls. Why would you say that?" I turn back and glance at my drinking buddy who hasn't lifted her head off the shiny bar for the past ten minutes.

"Because you said..." He makes a strangled sound in the back of his throat as I blink at his pretty face.

"So you thought I was a lesbo?"

"No, you told me that you…" His hands flail through the air and every few moments he makes a fist and gnashes his lips together into a silent snarl. He's so cute when he's mad. There's a little wrinkle at the corner of each eye, like a baby crow's foot. I bet Nate was cute as a baby, with fat cheeks and dark wavy hair. Those big blue eyes are perfect. I'm staring into them and can't remember why I was mad.

Nate takes my face in his palms and pivots my head until I'm looking at him. I giggle, "Hello."

"Kerry, how much did you drink?" He turns his head back to the bar and then down at me. "You're not even twenty-one, are you?"

I shake my head and grin. "Emily bought. I'm her responsibility."

Nate glances past me and frowns. "Since Emily is passed out on the bar, I'm thinking that was a bad plan."

"Emily is really pretty. I want to be pretty." Nate is ushering me back toward my spot at the bar. I'm about to sit down and start drinking my new pretty glass of tea when Nate pulls it out of my hands.

"Definitely not." He gets the bartender's attention and plays keep away with the glass.

"It's mine."

"You'll fall on your face," Nate says, holding it out of arm's reach.

Emily sits up with a napkin stuck to the side of her cheek, and gasps, "Don't let her near the stairs!" Her head immediately returns to the bar top with a thud.

I throw my arm around her shoulders and giggle so hard I can't stand up. "That was the funniest thing I've ever heard!"

"Come on, ladies." Nate is prying me off of Emily. He helps her up, lacing one arm under her shoulder and around her waist, leaving the other hand free to help usher me out the door.

As we pass a couch at the back of the room, a slender woman with wild red hair smiles up at Nate. "I had no idea you were a white knight, too, rescuing silly college girls from themselves." Her voice is deep and confident. It's how I hope I'll sound one day when I'm grown up. I keep waiting for it to happen—to be an adult.

The room is spinning. I say laughingly, "Someone has to do it."

She frowns. "Nice sweatpants."

"Thanks, an orphanage in Guam has my entire wardrobe. Like all of it."

She arches a perfectly plucked brow at me. But it's Nate who replies, surprised. "Really?"

I nod once and nearly puke, so I keep my mouth shut.

Nathan's reaction to my clothing disaster is interrupted by the chick he was probably making out with before he prevented me from falling down a stairwell. "Until next time." She lifts her glass and winks at him.

His face lights up.

I hate her.

CHAPTER 4

After we tuck Emily into her bed—at least I hope it was her bed—Nate takes me back to his little brownstone on the edge of the city. Austin is a weird place. Though the city sprawls across the land, spread out in a way New York could never be, it still has enough traffic to jam up the streets at any time of the day or night.

I'm sitting on Nate's couch with a cup of water in my hands. He's been telling me to drink it for the past however long I've been sitting here. I keep thinking about his rosy face and puffy lips.

He didn't want me.

Nate is sitting on the coffee table across from me, leaning forward, with his elbows on his knees and his hands folded together. His face is strong, and his jaw has a dusting of dark stubble. It makes his eyes appear brighter, bluer. I could look at him forever. The man is a masterpiece of beauty wrapped up in an irresistible body. Then there's his mind, painting abilities, and his sexy smirk. He's completely swoon-worthy, even after repetitive rejections.

Nate tips his head and points at my glass. "Drink up or you'll have a nasty hangover. You won't be able to tell off your ex tomorrow."

My mind is still on a conversation from a few hours ago. "Were you sucking face with that woman? She wanted you."

"I know." He doesn't elaborate.

I frown. "Why won't you tell me?"

"Because it doesn't matter. I was there for the same reason you were."

"Beer?"

He laughs, "No, to forget all the shit that didn't go right and stop thinking for the night. I knew you guys went drinking, but that place isn't the norm for college kids. They usually go further up the street."

"We heard the place was haunted."

"Of course. You were looking for ghosts. Well, my night was progressing fine, but then I saw you and—hell. What was I supposed to do?"

"You were supposed to keep me with you. You were supposed to get rid of the redhead and suck face with me." Holy fuck, why did I say that? I blink rapidly, not believing the room is still spinning. I pinch my forehead and try to put the water down.

Nate shoves it back into my hand. "I'm going to force-feed you that if you don't swallow soon."

With a droll expression on my face, I say, "That's what he said."

"Kerry!" Nate tries not to laugh, but can't help it. "You have no idea what you do to me." He cups my face between his hands as he says it, looking into my eyes.

Unfortunately, I can't hold his gaze long without the threat of ralphing on his shoes. "Likewise."

"Here," he's more gentle this time and holds up the glass, lifting it to my lips. "Only a little at a time."

Before I can say no, he tips up the glass and cool water rushes past my lips. Some spills down my chin and drips into my shirt while the rest slips over my lips and into my mouth. I swallow softly and remain perfectly still—wondering if he'll do it again.

He keeps the glass by my lips, and with his other hand, smooths the water over my neck. "Sorry, that must be cold."

I'm lost, watching him, wishing for more and knowing I'll never get it. Why do I keep chasing men who are bad for me? Nate is bad for me. Isn't he?

"Here, ready?" I nod. He lifts the glass again. When he lowers it, he wipes his thumb over my mouth, removing any beads of water still clinging to my lip. "That's not so bad, now is it?"

I don't answer. I watch him as he helps me again and again. The way his hands move and his gentle touch are crave-worthy. He smiles and speaks softly, his voice comforting. When his hand is on my neck and he tips the water to my lips, I nearly melt. I think about him trailing those warm hands down my throat and to my shoulder. I want him to pull me close and kiss me like he never wants to let go.

"What are you thinking about?" he asks. I've been quiet too long.

"Love. I used to think it was real, but I don't anymore."

His eyes cut to the side as he answers. "What made you decide that?"

"Because the concept of forever is flawed. Love is supposed to be this everlasting thing. If there is no forever, if nothing is certain—not even the love of a mother—then the entire concept is a lie." I blink slowly, watching him set the glass down across from me. "I don't like lies."

"Neither do I." His tone darkens, and he looks at his hands carefully. "I'd say you shouldn't judge your mother so harshly, but I see no point in that."

"Why?"

"Because mine did some atrocious things. Things horrible enough to stain the few memories I had of her forever. Ah, but there's your certainty of love. If hate can last for eternity, then surely love is possible."

"Possible, not probable."

He nods in agreement. "Unfortunately."

"So you want to be in love? You want forever?" I'm kind of surprised we're having this conversation, but I like it. Maybe he thinks I won't remember in the morning. Either way, he's forthcoming and doesn't have his walls up. It's nice.

He shakes his head and shrugs. "I have no idea what I want anymore. For a long time, no— love wasn't on my radar, and if I stumbled across it, I got the hell out of there."

"And now?" I look up into his beautiful face and hang on his words.

"Now, I have the urge to run."

My stomach twists. "Will you?"

His eyes are locked with mine and the intensity of his gaze makes me want to look away, but I can't. There's something so forlorn in his gaze, sadness that never retreated, darkness that stole nearly all his light. I want to know what made him this way.

"No. Nothing could chase me away from you." He's so close to me and in that moment, everything feels surreal. It's as if a moment went missing from time. I feel the draw to him, the insatiable desire to touch his skin and feel his body on mine. I blink slowly, not wanting to miss a thing. Nate lingers there, head hung between his shoulders, his eyes locked on mine so long I think he's not going to do anything. Certainly he senses this incredible attraction between us. It can't be only me.

Just when I drop my gaze, I feel his finger under my chin. He tips my head back and, before I can ask what's wrong, his lips are on mine. It's a whisper of a kiss at first, but it quickly changes to something darker, something raw and unfettered. His mouth presses against mine, his tongue slipping between my lips, demanding more. He moans into my mouth as he stands and towers over me, holding my face, moving me where he wants me.

Nate presses me back into the couch, kissing me harder and straddling my lap. His hands are everywhere, touching, gripping, and holding me. I writhe beneath him wanting more, wishing there were no clothes between us. I tug his hair hard and drink him in, intoxicated with every bit of him. His scent fills my head and leaves me utterly breathless. I want him to ravage me. I want that feeling of oneness with him as he drives into me.

I press my hips up into his and arch my back against him. He's breathing hard in my ear as he starts kissing my neck. His hands slide up my back, under my shirt, and he holds on tight. The bulge that's rocking into me is becoming harder to ignore. I'm near mindless, purring into his kisses and begging him for more.

Slowly, he pulls away. "I want this too—so much, but not like this. Not tonight."

"Nate," I reach for him as he stands. "I can't believe you're rejecting me again." I'm close to crying, and beyond ashamed.

"Kerry, I want to be with you," he smiles down at me and gently explains, "but you're a little wasted. I don't want to take advantage of that. I don't want you ever to think I'd do something like that. Don't cry."

I don't answer. I can't. The lump in my throat is the size of a bowling ball and choking me.

He turns and trails his fingers down my forearm and into my palm, lacing his fingers with mine before tilting his head to the side and saying, "Come with me."

"Where are we going?"

"To bed."

CHAPTER 5

My arm is draped over my throbbing head as I slowly wake up. There's a hammering in my head that won't stop. The sandy sensation in my mouth isn't cool either. I try to remember what I was doing that lead to this, and vividly recall going to the haunted bar with Emily. After that it gets fuzzy. I was hungry and ate Long Island Iced Teas for dinner instead of food. God, I need a drink of water. I try to swallow, but my throat is too dry.

Water. There's a ping of a memory floating around in the back of my head. I didn't want water and someone with nice hands was a total pusher.

The memories break through my hangover haze as they bust through the floodgates of my mind. You know those blinders that are attached to your brain that tell you something you did was so dumbass stupid that it refuses to take credit for it? Well, they break away, and I remember.

"Oh, crap," I groan and drop my arm from my face. I squint away from the sunlight and feel some pity for vampires who have to walk around like that all the time. They're commonly mistaken for nearsighted citizens. Squinting is not sexy.

Neither am I at the moment. I'm aware of my actions last night but too horrified to face Nate. The guy has got to think I'm insane. Speaking of Nate, I glance around and notice I'm in his bed alone. The spot next to me is wrinkle-free, and the bedspread still has neatly folded hospital corners.

The little room has yellow oak floors and white walls. A few articles of clothing litter the floor near a dresser in the corner with a TV on top. There's a painting he made hanging over my head. I want to crane my neck to see it, but my brain is trying to claw its way out of my skull.

A floorboard creaks and Nate appears with a tray in his hands. He rounds the bed to the messy side and sets the tray on a nightstand.

"Good morning, beautiful." He's grinning down at me. He's so freaking shiny I can barely look at him.

"It's not nice to tease people."

"I'm not, it's the truth. I've never seen a more seductive woman in my life." He's grinning now, and I can't help it, my face starts burning. "That show you put on was something else."

Fuck it. If you do something stupid, own it. I push up on an elbow, and my knotty hair falls over my shoulder. "Sexy, right?"

"Very."

"Especially the way I curved and moved."

"Not to mention the kiss."

I manage to keep my expression neutral. "Ah, yes, well that was in a league of its own."

"Entirely." If he smiles any wider, his ears won't fit on his head.

The corners of my lips twist up into a lopsided grin. "So, before last night, you were a total virgin, am I right?"

"For that particular scenario, yes. I can't say I've ever done anything like that."

Score for Kerry! Be unforgettable, by choice or by accident. It's all the same in the end. I'm the crazy chick. "I can't say I remember doing that either."

"Mmmm." That sound is close to a purr in the back of this throat. "Good. I like that I'm the only one who's seen you flying your freak flag."

"That was nothing. There's all sorts of crazy crap going on up here." I tap the side of my head and wince.

"Seriously, though. It was like a sexy Cirque du Soleil performance… with socks."

I can't help it, I laugh. So last night may have taken an unexpected turn. I remember heading to his bedroom and ditching my sweatpants after seeing a pair of his argyle socks on the dresser. While these actions aren't logical to a sober person, my drunken self considered it totally normal. I might have pulled on a pair and tugged those suckers up to my knees, then started dancing around the room. I moved like a ballerina with no pants and no gloves, wearing only panties, a bra, and my t-shirt.

"Ah, yes. Well, you can't dance without a pair of kickass gloves." For some reason gloves were very important, so I ditched my shirt (because that makes sense), and pulled on a second pair of his polka dot socks over my hands and up my arms. They were my opera gloves. I was very proud.

"Obviously." He grins so hard a dimple appears on his cheek. It's impossibly sexy and sweet. The man is hot and I was dancing through his room, plastered. "The puppet show was really something. I can't say I've ever enjoyed watching a girl kiss a sock before."

Oh, God. I forgot about that part. Mortified I try to slide under the sheets, but Nate kneels on the floor next to the bed and peers underneath.

"Actually, I've never wanted to be a sock so much in my life." His dark hair falls in his eyes as he smiles at me.

"He got more action than you."

"By far."

"I made out with your socks and then passed out on your bed?" It's a question because the night gets super fuzzy after that.

"You did."

My eyes cut to the side and then back to his beautiful face. "And you'd like me to leave now?"

"Hell, no. That was the most amazing evening I've had in a long time."

I laugh lightly. "Dude, you need to get out more."

Nate pulls back the sheet and sits on the edge of the bed. "You need to let your freak flag fly a little more frequently. You're like a repressed schoolgirl who never did anything bad."

I avoid his gaze and play with the hem of the sheet. "That's a fairly accurate statement."

"I like sexy sock girl."

I grin sheepishly and tease, "You would."

Nate places his hands on either side of my head and leans in close. His lips linger just above mine as he watches me. "Want to do something crazy?"

No. Yes! Maybe. All three answers must flash across my face based on the way he chortles. It's an amazing sound. It's pure joy mixed with this deep tone that caresses me in all the right places.

Nate continues, "No masks. No hiding. Instead of waiting months, or however long it takes to really get to know someone, lets start there. The more I see the real you, the more I like you."

Warning bells are going off in my head. IT'S A TRAP! SAY, FUCK NO! THEN RUN AWAY! And take his socks with you to remember him by. See? I can't say shit like that out loud. He'll run away screaming.

My heart is hammering hard, slamming into my lungs and making it hard to breathe. Nate is right there, so close I can feel the warmth from his breath slip over my lips.

He tips his forehead forward and presses it to mine. "You're over thinking this."

"You haven't thought about it enough."

"Life is short. This cuts out all the crap and just leaves us with two real, raw people."

"Have you seen raw people? They're a mess."

"I know and I trust you." He leans a little closer and presses a kiss to the tip of my nose. "I'll tell you what I'm thinking, uncensored, if you agree to do the same. Would you like to hear a secret?"

I swallow hard wishing he'd press his chest to mine and ravage me. Instead, I barely move and can't seem to get my voice to work. I'm terrified that my breath smells like dead hamsters. He doesn't seem to notice. Maybe he has an olfactory issue and can't smell anything? It's not fair because he's perfect, already showered and dressed with that cologne that makes me want to slide my hands all over his naked body and lick him from head to toe.

See? I can't say that to him. If I did, who knows what would happen.

"There's this little spot at the nape of your neck that has this silky soft skin combined with this beautiful curve that I've been dying to taste again." He trails his finger over the spot, making me shiver.

"I don't think this is a good idea." I try to sit up, but he won't let me.

"Ask me anything. I'll tell you."

I'm watching his face, looking into his eyes and I know he's serious. The pit of my stomach is in a free-fall, and this makes me feel too vulnerable. It's exhilarating and intimidating at the same time. I press my lips together, suck in a deep breath, and decide to jump.

"Okay, I'll bite. Why'd you leave me the night we met? The phone rang, and you dropped me and walked away." I try to avoid his eyes when I'm asking him because it still bothers me. I felt like trash that night after the way he treated me.

"My father died. I was in that hotel room waiting for the call. He was working up in New York and got in a nasty accident. An eighteen-wheeler hit his car—he flipped. I knew I'd have to go up there, but I didn't want to be on a plane when he died. It's stupid, I know. I'd gone to the hotel because I didn't want those memories in this house. I went a little stir crazy, so I headed to the bar to get some fresh air. I'd been sitting in the room all day. That's when you came over. Between the incident in the bathroom and then again at the bar, I didn't know what to think of you, but you had my full attention. I wanted to spend the night with you and forget everything, but it didn't work out that way. I should have never taken you back with me. I'm so sorry, Kerry."

Nate sits back on the bed and rubs the heels of his hands over his eyes, before dropping them and glancing at me.

"I'm sorry. I had no idea." I push up in the bed and lean back against the headboard. "Ask me anything. It's AMA day with Kerry Hill. All crazy. All the time."

Nate glances at me from under dark lashes. His hands are folded together, and his legs are hanging over the edge of the bed. "That first day when you walked into the men's room, why were you crying?"

I smile, but it falls swiftly. "Ah, yeah. That day was rough. I got text-dumped by my boyfriend. He'd promised me forever, but I hadn't been here a week when he said it was over. He met someone else."

Nate nods slowly. "And from what you said before, it sounds like the other woman is your mother?"

I pinch the bridge of my nose and nod. "Yeah. They're arriving today. I'm supposed to act like it doesn't bother me even though it feels like I still have two knives lodged between my shoulder blades."

"So, you seriously were looking for sex with no strings attached that night in the bar?"

"Yeah."

"Did you find it? I mean after that?"

I shake my head. "No. I keep getting turned down. It's like a guy can smell the crazy coming his way. I never had a chance."

"That's not it."

I glance over at him. He sounds so certain, so sure there's another reason. "Really? After the sock dance of sexiness, you're still convinced it's something else."

He grins and laughs. "Yes, with one hundred percent accuracy. I know why guys won't go near you, even in sweats. It's simple, and it's amplified by the fact that you have no idea."

"If you're waiting for me to have an epiphany and suddenly get what you're saying, you're going to be disappointed." I blink at him and hold up my palms, shrugging. "I have no clue."

"I know. That's what makes you over-the-top, drop-dead, completely sexy. You're an unattainable goddess. Nothing can hide that. Every man wants you and hardly any have the guts to talk to you. And if you try to seduce one, well, he feels average in comparison to you."

I'm gaping at him. "What? No, I'm not. I think you need glasses, Smitty."

Nate shakes his head. "Nope. That's not even the most intimidating part."

"There's more?"

That dimple reappears when he speaks. "Yes, and this is the reason why you can't find a rebound guy. A woman like you, a woman so irresistibly sexy has got to want a man of equal allure in bed. They think they're outmatched."

I snort and jab a finger at the socks lying on the floor. "By the sock monster? I don't think so."

He leans in and whispers in my ear. "I won't lie to you. Every bit of it is true."

"And you?" I turn to him and look into those blue eyes. "Are you afraid of me?"

"I'd be an idiot if I wasn't intimidated by you. You're incredibly sexy, smart, and determined.

The more I know of you, the more I want to know. That night we were together was just a glimpse of what it would be like to be with you. I want that. You're worth risking everything." Nate closes the distance between us and presses his lips to my cheek.

He takes his hands and slides them up my arms until he's cradling my head. When he tips it to the side, he lowers his mouth onto my neck, into the curve he was talking about earlier. His lips are hot and slick as he kisses that spot. My lashes lower and I suck in a jagged breath. Every inch of me wants this, wants him, but I can't fathom what he's told me.

I'm not that pretty. I've seen myself. I know. Why would any guy think that about me? I'm normal, average, with incredibly crappy luck. I mean, there's a hot guy sucking on my neck and I want to melt into him, but at the same time, his words worry me. If he wanted to use me, he could have. If there was a time to lie to me, it's in the past. He didn't have to say those things to be with me.

Unnerved, I pull away and press back into the headboard. Breathless, I ask, "Can we slow down?"

Nate nods slowly and looks up at me. "Anything you want."

I manage a fake smile and nod. "It's just that this feels like more than a random hookup. It wasn't supposed to. It was supposed to be a one-night thing, a fuckable evening with a hot guy. Instead, it feels like you're in my head." And working your way into my heart. I can't deal with that. I don't want anyone there, not for a long time.

"If it's any consolation, you're in mine too. All day and night. All thoughts keep returning to you. I can't help it, and it's not something I wanted either."

His words are brutally honest, unguarded. I glance up at him. "Then what are we doing?"

"I don't know." He slips out of bed and paces the floor for a moment, running his hands down his neck. His tight t-shirt clings to his body and his dark jeans hug his hips as he walks. He's so perfect, so beautiful, and so closed off from the rest of the world. For some reason, he decided to speak to me, and I'm jacking it up.

Nate stops and glances over at me. "I don't want to see you upset, and I know today is going to be hard for you. I meant it when I said I'd be your friend. I'm getting the vibe that you're a loner despite all the friends you've made. There's no one you completely lean on or trust."

"After what's happened, can you blame me?"

"No, not at all. Life takes its toll, Kerry. Just don't shut everyone out. You can't survive alone. Believe me, I know. I've tried." Nate's body tenses and his jaw locks. It's like he's ready to fight something I can't see. He's thinking of something specific—something he lived through. Even though it's over, it's still haunting him.

CHAPTER 6

After I shower and pull on another sweat suit—this one is Nate's and really big—I check my messages. Beth left about twenty voicemails starting with a chipper 'let's go shopping' to the frantic, 'are you dead in a ditch' message. I need to call her.

I punch in her number. When she picks up, I hear a variety of creative threats followed by shrill swearing.

"I'm sorry, Beth. I went out with Emily and ran into Nate."

Beth sounds like she's panting. "Nate? As in the hot teacher man?"

"Yeah. What are you doing?"

"Running."

"Since when do you run?"

"Since I decided I wanted to wear catsuits and I realized my ass is too big. Stay on point," she huffs. "You went home with Nate?"

"Yeah, sorta."

"There is no sorta. Where are you now?"

"At his house."

"Holy shit! Did you sleep with him?"

"Stop asking that question."

"Well, it's important! It tells me how crazy you are. That guy is risking everything for you. Either that or he's insane and doesn't care if he loses his job."

"No, that's not it. He likes me."

"Awh, how sweet. So are you going to fuck him or not?"

"Beth!"

"Listen, bitch. We were supposed to go shopping, so get your ass back over here and let's find you something that will make him drool."

He's already drooling. I want to tell her, but it sounds weird to tell another woman that Nate said I'm a goddess. From what I can tell, he thinks it too. I don't know what to do with that. So, I agree, hoping it'll make things more normal. "Sounds good. I'll meet you at the mall."

CHAPTER 7

Nate is really sweet. He offers to drive me, rescuing me from driving the bus with the beast in back. It's the little things that make me a happy camper.

When we pull into the parking lot, he drives up to the entrance where I agreed to meet Beth. Nate watches me gather my things. "I meant what I said before. You're beautiful."

I smile awkwardly and nod. "Thank you?" Damn it. It wasn't supposed to sound like a question.

Nate grabs my hand and squeezes it. "I'll see you later, okay?"

"Yeah." Just before I let go of his hand, he pulls me in and kisses me softly on the mouth.

It was totally unexpected. I gasp when he pulls away, which makes him cock his head to the side and consider me.

"I took your breath away?"

"Literally." I can't Hoover in air fast enough.

He laughs and lightly runs his finger over the back of my hand. "I look forward to seeing what other sexy sounds you make."

I laugh like that will never happen, but I'm not entirely sure what's up with him or me anymore. Stop over thinking it, Kerry. He doesn't want a relationship and neither do you. It's a good time and that's it. It's friends by day and fuckbuddies by night—minus the sock show. What the hell was I thinking?

I wink at him and walk away. Beth is perched by the doors, and apparently watched the entire exchange. "Classy. Very nice flirty thing you had going on there."

I tuck my hair behind my ear. I haven't felt like myself since I got to Texas. I'm constantly wearing borrowed clothes, and I feel frumpy. "Really?"

Beth's head jerks back and she says, "Psh, hell yeah! I'd do you. I mean it was that hot. He's eating out of your hand, and totally wishes he was eating out—"

My eyes bug out of my head as she talks. It's loud enough that a few passersby pause to stare at us. I cover her mouth before she can say the rest. "Beth! Cut it out!"

She pulls away. "Oh, you're no fun. You can't do it if you can't talk about it." She waves a finger at me and sounds like she's giving me 'the talk.'

"I'm mature enough, Mom. I promise."

She grins. "You better be, because I want details. That man is hot."

Nodding, I agree, "He is. The thing is—"

She grabs me by the crook of my arm and tugs me toward the stores. "No. There is no thing, no problem, no nothing. He's crazy about you and willing to get fired to fuck you. And you think he's super hot. Remember, you bet cake? It's time to eat the cake, Kerry."

She stops in front of Victoria's Secret and stares up at the window display. There are three lace teddies. The center one is rich red with a plunging neckline that goes all the way to the navel. The back is even more revealing with a piece of string at the center back strap and a G-string. That's it.

"I'm more of a babydoll kind of girl." I say staring at the display.

"Not anymore. This is makeover day. You're not leaving here without something sexy."

I frown and follow her into the store. "Babydolls are sexy."

"Yeah, if you're a virgin, which you're not. And there's no way in hell he is, so stop pretending you have no clue how smoking hot you are and get something that's on the level you want to be." Beth starts looking through racks of bras. She pulls one out and studies the fabric.

"Pretend for a second that you make no sense." I give her a big dorky grin. I didn't go shopping for sex clothes when I was with Matt. I got bras and panties, but not a fuck-me outfit.

Beth sighs and puts the bra back. "Geeze. Fine, I'll show you myself. The super slutty stuff is always toward the back of the store. Here." She stops in front of a display, which looks tame. "Yeah, not that. Turn around."

When I pivot, I'm facing a nook with lots of sheer fabric, lace, and strings. "I can't wear something like that."

Beth folds her arms over her chest and taps her foot. "What kind of night do you want to have with him? Sweet? Chaste kisses and giggles? Then get a babydoll. If you want to have the hottest sex of your life, you need clothing that says so. Like this stuff." She pulls out three outfits on hangers and pushes them at me.

"Beth, this is seriously a bad idea." One of the price tags catches my eye and I nearly choke. "I can't buy these. It'll use up my entire paycheck for just one."

"Money well spent, newbie. Go pick one out. Take selfies."

I frown as I stumble toward the fitting room. "What for?"

Beth laughs and shakes her head. "Just do it. I'll show you later."

A sales girl opens a room for me and hangs up the barely there clothing. "Let me know if you need anything else."

"Thanks." I close the door as she leaves and look in the mirror. I'm a frumpy mess with frizzed-out hair and too-big sweats.

I hesitate, not wanting to put these on. What kind of person does that make me? I'm sweet and pretty. That's how I see myself.

That's not how Nate sees me at all.

A goddess would wear this stuff. Actually, a goddess would walk around naked and rock it. Since I can't pull that off, maybe this isn't that bad. You'd think the line between modesty and nude model wouldn't be miles apart in my mind, but they are. One is art and the other is sex. They don't merge and they never mingle.

After I strip, I try to put on the first teddy. It covers my body like a swimsuit, but it's made of lace, so it's sheer in a lot of places. The girls have no support and I don't like the way the crotch appears to be eating my hips. It's just weird. I pull it off and try another. Same thing. It's not me.

Beth comes in, hollering, "I have a few more. Where are you?"

"Over here." As I crack open the door, she shoves a few more hangers at me.

"That pink one is kind of retro. I thought it was cool."

I glance down at it. I can't tell what it's supposed to look like. There's more fabric than the other outfits, so it's ahead on that account. I try the next teddy and the next body suit. They aren't right. I don't feel sexy. I feel like someone else. That is, until I try on the last one—the retro looking, light pink, lacy teddy. It has a wire in the cup, cut-away sides, and dashes of lace on a sheer bodice. The shoulders are thin straps, like a bra, and the back dips down to my waist. There are linear stripes of pink satin and then one horizontal stripe at the waist, like a belt, with a little bow in front. It makes my waist look tiny and my hips look killer curvy. The girls are up and the placement of the lace and stripes hides my nips. It's weird how little things like that help me find my spine because I do. I straighten up and can see me owning this. I could strut in this, in heels and thigh highs. My hair could be blown out, smooth, and I can picture me wearing it, and then not wearing it.

My daydream is interrupted by soft giggles coming from the next changing room. "Shhh, they'll hear you."

A male voice whispers back, "You know you like getting caught."

TMI. I slip out of the piece of lingerie and feel happy. I won't have money to buy jeans or Pringles for another week, but sex clothes come first, right? And if things go to hell, I can pretend this is a shirt. It'll look great with sweatpants.

As I slip into my clothes, there are noises coming from the next room and a steady moan, tap, moan combo. He must be fucking her on the little bench and it raps the wall with every thrust. Despite their attempts to be quiet, they're far from it.

When I bend over to grab my shoes, a flash of blonde hair catches my eye. There, upside down and facing me is the woman who held me in her arms and kissed away my boo-boos. Her mouth is covered in slutty red lipstick and forms a perfect O. Her eyes are closed as she purrs. She must be leaning over the bench for me to see her face, which means he's banging her from behind.

I panic. I don't want to finish the thought. I don't want to picture Matt butt fucking my mother in a changing room. I make a strangled sound and pull my shoe on as fast as I can.

Mom's eyes flash open and she sees me. "Kerry!"

I'm not seeing this. This isn't happening. I grab my bag and run from the dressing room with one sneaker in my hand and the other on my foot. The sales girl looks concerned when I come racing out, face flushed.

"Are you all right?"

"Yeah, fine." I push past her and dart out the front of the store without waiting for Beth. I race down a corridor off the main hallway and grab a bench behind a potted plant that's huge and can hide me. I bury my face in my hands and try not to cry or scream.

It's not right. It's not fair. It's fucking wrong! I'm leaning forward, rocking gently, and growling into my hands by the time Beth finds me. "What the hell was that?" She plops down next to me.

I flip my hair out of my face and offer a plastic smile of indifference. "Matt was doing my mother in the dressing room next to mine. Isn't it a lovely day?"

Beth glances back down the way she came. "Are you serious?"

I nod and bury my face in my hands. "I saw her. Do you know how horrible it is to see your parents having sex?"

She grimaces. "Unfortunately, I do."

"Now add your first love to the mix and see where that gets you. How am I supposed to be okay with this? They're both assholes!" I stand up and shake my hands in the air as if that might help.

Beth stands next to me. "They are, and you know what—you don't need them. You still have your dad and your siblings. You shouldn't keep people around you that are toxic and this is like munching on poisoned pops for kicks. Kerry, there's only so much suckage a girl can take."

"I know and I'm past it. I'm over the limit."

"So, go back there and tell her. Hell, tell them off."

"I will." I jump up and rush back the way I came, formulating a plan in my mind. I walk straight to the back of the store and grab the piece of lingerie I wanted. I walk over to the line at the cash register and stand there, knowing she'll come to me.

A few moments later, there they are, all sweaty and freshly fucked. My mom puts her hand on the small of my back. "Honey, I thought we lost you."

I turn and she drops her hand. I manage to pry open my locked jaw and speak. "Oh, hi. I didn't see you there."

She glances at my hanger dangling from my index finger, making it easy to see. "Is that for a new boyfriend?"

Smiling, I shake my head. "Nope. It's for a frat party. Slave girl auction."

She blanches. "You're going to wear that to a frat party?"

I shrug. "Yeah, of course. What else would I wear?" I don't say anything else and turn around.

Just then Josh spots me and rushes over. He whispers in my ear, "Beth told me. I'll play along. Do your worst."

I swat at him. "Later. You have to bid like the other guys. It's too skanky to do it in the dressing room."

Josh feigns insult. "That's not what you said last night."

My eyes narrow, cutting to the side as the corner of my lips pulls into a sly grin. "Oh, that's right. I said that to your brother, too."

Josh's jaw drops. "Which one? Justin? Jace?"

"Kerry," Mom tries shoving between us to butt in. "Who is your little friend?"

She wants an introduction. Is she kidding me? As if this wasn't bad enough, Matt struts up behind her and places a hand on her shoulder. He peers down at me with pity. Asshole.

I put my arm around Josh's waist and pull him in tight. "This is my fuckbuddy. Josh, this is my mom and my ex-douche of a boyfriend, Matt. Soon he'll be my dad and it'll be like Sister Wives, but with my mom!" I feign excitement then turn around, not waiting for a reply.

I feel bad for hurting her because she's my mother and it clearly does. But I don't understand how she could choose him over me. At the end of the day, that was her decision and she has to live with it. Unfortunately, so do I. As soon as they ring me up and put my stuff in the pink bag, I leave with Josh on my arm.

CHAPTER 8

Once we're back to the bench where I left Beth, I fill her in and thank Josh. "I really appreciated that."

"I wish it were true, especially since you bought that." He inclines his head toward the bag.

I laugh. "You wish."

"I do. I've never denied it."

Beth glares at him. "No shagging my friends! You promised. Stop looking at her and pick someone else."

I glance up and catch the worry in Josh's eyes. Beth doesn't know about the hotel room. No one does. He's thinking the same thing, and I know without a doubt, he'll make sure his little sister is happy above everything else.

He teases her a little more by sauntering over to me and dipping me back in his arms. "Hey, sexy. Want to have a good time?"

I giggle. "Not with you."

He straightens and covers his heart with his hand as if I'd shot him. He staggers backward and says, "That was brutal."

Beth folds her arms over her chest, taps her foot, and glares at Josh. "It's not half as brutal as I'll be if you mess with her."

"I'm just teasing, Beth. Kerry is like a sister to me, an incredibly, bodacious, succulent, sinful...what was I saying?" He flashes a grin my way, then waggles his eyebrows at Beth. "You worry too much." He leans in and kisses Beth's forehead, before strutting off. He calls back over his shoulder, "And Kerry, send me a picture of your new outfit. I'd love to give you some fashion tits. I mean tips."

I frown and look over at Beth. "You seriously have nothing to worry about."

"Yeah, well, weirder things have happened."

I smack her arm with the back of my hand, lightly to get her attention. I point toward her brother. "That is never going to happen."

CHAPTER 9

Beth drives me to Nate's without commenting further on Josh. I know it worries her, and I really wish it didn't. I have a love-hate thing with Josh. He's a tease—and so insincere he has no idea which way is up anymore.

I walk into the kitchen and find Nate at the little table. He's holding a letter in his hands with the envelope still sealed. "So, this came in the mail." He taps the paper against his other hand.

I pull out a chair and sit down, tucking my bag away so he can't see it. "What is it?"

"I don't know." He's staring at the envelope like it's filled with anthrax.

"Do you want me to open it?"

He glances past the paper in his hands and into my eyes. There's so much emotion swirling bitterly beneath the surface it scares me. Something is very wrong and he thinks it's going to get worse. Nate hands me the envelope. "Open it."

I hesitate for a moment, then rip it open. I fish out the paper and unfold it. It's from a law firm in New York and it's addressed to him. My lips move as I silently read the words until I come to the part he's dreading. I glance up at him over the top of the paper. "What do you know about this?"

From the look on his face, he's already aware of the situation. "A little. Peter Ferro was carrying a letter claiming my dad wasn't my biological father, that I was actually the byproduct of an affair between my mother and Peter Ferro's father. I didn't believe it, so I told the firm they were mistaken. That's their response, isn't it?"

I nod slowly. I can tell this has shaken him to the core. "You had no idea?"

"No." His elbows are on the table and his head hangs between his shoulders as his hands fist next to his ears. He doesn't look up at me. "Tell me what it says."

I scan the paper again and try to summarize it in a way that won't be like a bat to the groin. "It says that your father loved you, and his death triggered a few things. One was a full background work up on you because of a paternity test your mother had done a long time ago. There was a clause in her will that was dormant until your father passed away. When that happened two letters were issued. One to you and one to Mr. Ferro stating he had a son and one telling you that you weren't alone. That you still had family."

"Those people are not my family." He growls as he tugs his hair hard.

"They included the paternity test company and a copy of the results. They are also saying that there was money set aside, a trust." I scan it a few times to make sure I understand what they're saying before I tell him. "It sounds like there's an inheritance."

"I know—he had the house. This one. There was nothing else." Nate sits up and stares at me. His lips mash together and he slams his hands on the table. "Damn it! I hate this, Kerry. I don't know what the hell to do. I can't stand the thought of my mother being unfaithful, but here I am—living proof she screwed some other guy. The fact that it's that Ferro douche-bag makes it so much worse." He's up pacing before he finishes speaking. "I don't want their money. I don't want anything to do with them."

This is really weird. Growing up in New York, I heard rumors about the Ferros all the time—it would've been impossible not to hear stuff. Everyone seems fascinated by the Ferro family, and they can't seem to stay out of the news for one reason or another. But I never expected to find a tie to them in Texas, let alone something like this.

Nate is the secret Ferro bastard baby. As far as I know, there are no other illegitimate children despite Mr. Ferro's philandering for decades and fucking multiple fertile young women. Nate is a few years older than Jonathan Ferro, closer to Peter's age. He has brothers, half-brothers.

"Nate?" He turns to look at me, wild-eyed. "What did Peter want?"

"I don't know. To make sure I got the letter, I suppose."

I nod slowly. "I wish I knew what to say to make it better. God knows I'd douse myself with a good shot of it too. Then everything bad would disappear and we could be happy."

Nate walks over to me without the slightest hesitation and presses his lips to mine. He tangles his fingers in my hair and firmly holds me in place. After the day I've had, I want to get lost in him. The desperate nature of his kiss makes it more carnal and raw. He forces his tongue into my mouth and then takes a few steps forward, slamming me into the wall.

Don't think. Just feel.

The heat coming off his body is intense. The scent of him fills my head as I grab his shirt and pull him closer. The kiss feels frantic and it's impossible to breathe. My heart races harder as his hands drop to the hem of the oversized shirt and slip beneath it. His warm palms are on my stomach and then my back. He slips them up and pulls me closer to him as he does it, never breaking the kiss.

Nate tastes every crevice of my mouth and every time I try to take control of the kiss he forces me back. When his teeth nip my lip, I squeak a little yelp. An erotic smile spreads across his lips for a moment. "Do that again." He says the words while pressing his lips against my mouth.

When I don't reply, he nips me and the sound repeats. Nate pulls away for half a second and looks up and down at me. I'm against the kitchen wall, huffing like a beast. Things weren't supposed to happen this way. I bought lingerie. It's still in the bag under the table.

Through jagged breaths, Nate manages to ask, "Tell me how you want it. Gentle, slow?"

I shake my head. "No. I want…" I suck in air and feel my breasts rise, swelling as my body fills with lust.

Nate steps toward me, his eyes darkening, the flash of blue burning bright. "Say it. Tell me what you want."

"You. I want you—rough, raw, and messy. I don't want gentle. Not now."

Nate grins wolfishly and I gasp as he crushes me to the wall, kissing me harder than before. There's nothing slow or gentle about it. He's angry, and so am I. I want to be with him and this mood suits me well. All the emotions I've had trapped beneath the surface can rush out. I don't have to hold back, not with him.

Nate paws at my shirt until he rips it off and tosses it on the floor. The bra follows and I stay there, topless, pinned to the wall by his hard body. He forces his knee between my legs and dips his head to that spot on my neck. His hands cover my breasts as his thumbs find my nipples. He squeezes them hard, making me cry out. The sensation is intense and shoots straight between my legs. When he raises his head from my neck, he lowers his body, trailing kisses down my throat and to my breast. His lips suck as his tongue flicks and I tip my head back and cry out. My nails claw the wall as he teases me. After he sucks, flicks, and nips each breast, his tongue travels further down my chest, past my stomach and stops at my waist. Without warning, Nate tugs the waistband on the sweats and yanks them off with my panties in one movement.

I'm standing in his kitchen naked, pressed to the wall. Nate rises and reaches for his jeans, unbuttoning them and then lowering the zipper. I've not done it standing up, not like this. The lights are on and the windows are open allowing plenty of daylight to pour into the room. There's no hiding under covers, no careful, slow, exploration. That's for another time.

I reach for the hem of his shirt and tug it hard, pulling him toward me. "Fuck me, Nate. Make me forget my name. Make me scream for more."

A wicked grin spreads across his lips as he reaches into his pants and frees his hard shaft. He moans into my ear when he reaches for me. His lips are hot, and his voice is heavy with lust, "I love it when you talk like that."

He pulls a condom from his pocket and rips it open with his teeth. His knee forces apart my thighs and I find myself on my tippy-toes trying to rub against him. I'm so hot, and I want to be touched so badly. I writhe against his jeans for a moment and then let out a frustrated sigh. "Nate."

He answers in my ear, "Yeah baby?"

"I want you." I start to beg him. I don't plan to, it just happens.

Nate grabs my thigh with one hand and hooks my leg on his hip. With his other hand, he puts on the protection and positions himself low. There are no probing fingers, no gentle foreplay. It's straight to fucking. I tip my head back and try not to be impatient, but he's right there. When he stands, I feel him slide inside and gasp. He fills me and then some, pressing me in a way I haven't felt before. I pant and wrap my legs around his waist to try and hold myself in place. Nate catches my thighs in his hands and shifts me up, which makes me come down hard, and forces me to take all of him at once.

I make a high-pitched noise and then melt into him, eyes closed, lips parted, a coy smile on my face.

He grins, "You like that?"

I look at him through hooded eyes. "Yes."

"Tell me what you want, baby."

I bite my lower lip and know he won't move until I ask. He has the power, but he keeps giving it back to me at pivotal points. I like it. I want to say things, things I'd never say to anyone else. I start rocking my hips as I speak, "Don't move."

Nate groans and tips his head back. His eyes close for a second and his fingers dig into my legs. I slowly rock against him, pivoting my hips, and making cooing sounds each time. I want more. The slight, controlled movements backfire, making me want to ride him harder and feel him deeper. I whisper into his ear, telling him all the dirty things I want to do to him.

"Holy fuck, Kerry." Every inch of his body is tense muscle, waiting for my command to ravage me. I've never felt so powerful in life. His body shakes as he tries to hold it together, as he torments himself waiting for my directive.

I swing my hips up slowly, squeezing my muscles as I slide back down. When our eyes meet, I breathe the command, "Fuck me. Hard. Don't stop."

Nate shifts his hands further up my thighs, nearly to my ass, and digs his fingers in as he slams me back into the wall. All the air is forced from my lungs as he does it and he pushes deeper within me. I arch my back and push against him, creating a rhythm of his hips rocking into mine, forcing himself inside deeper, faster. The pace is fast and hard. There are going to be bruises all over my thighs tomorrow, but I don't care. It feels like I'm a goddess and he'll do anything he can to sate my lust. My heels dig into his jeans as he pushes again and again, harder and faster. His body is covered in sweat and his clothing is clinging to his toned muscles. He doesn't pause or slow.

My hands tangle in his hair as I lose myself in him. I can't fathom what I'm saying in those moments. I'm lost. I'm all sex and no thought. I want him. I need him. We slam together, purring, and fucking until those tightly coiled parts of me can't keep it together anymore. I shatter in his arms, as he pumps into me, not relinquishing his hold or slowing his pace. It does something I don't expect and I'm suddenly panting and breathless again, climbing higher, begging to be fucked harder, faster.

He laughs and coos my name. "Come for me, Kerry."

"I did." I'm lost again, floating somewhere between heaven and earth with no intention of coming down. The tightness inside coils again and grows bigger, quickly.

"Again. Come again." He drives into me as he grabs my thighs, and pulls them higher on his hips.

I can't think. My body is lost in a bliss that's pure and sinful. When Nate increases his speed and then slows, I lurch forward and claw his back through his shirt. Fucking fabric.

"You like that?" He moves against me again, slower. I can't tell what he's doing, but it leaves me unable to speak. I gasp again and again while frantically trying to come. I'm so close. He resumes his speed, breathless, and this time when he slows he slams in hard. Once, twice, and on the third time, I shatter in his arms for the second time.

CHAPTER 10

As I lay in his arms, everything else fades away. For a brief moment, I can pretend I'm all right. No memories haunt me. No regrets crush my heart. I'm focused on his warm body crushed against mine. Nate breathes steadily as he runs his fingers through my hair, his gaze on the ceiling. From the curve of his mouth, I know he's thinking about something unpleasant. His high is already gone. Life is so crushing he can't outrun it for more than a moment at a time.

I clear my throat and tip my head back, glancing up at him. That beautiful face looks down at me, and a cocky grin spreads across his kissable lips. "Hey, there." His voice is so deep it rumbles in his chest.

"Hey, yourself." After a moment, I see the happiness drain away from his face. "Put that smile back on right now."

"Is that a threat?"

"Yes."

"Or you'll do what?" The corner of his mouth pulls up into a lopsided grin as he shifts his weight to get a better look at me.

I don't let him move. "Or I'll climb right back up there and make you smile again."

He grins. "I like that threat."

I can't stop smiling. "You would."

"I noticed that little pink bag when you walked in earlier. What's in there? Something good?"

"Nope, something bad. Very bad."

"That sounds intriguing."

"It is, and you know what?"

Before he can answer, the ding-dong of the doorbell sounds. I dart upright, clutching the sheet to my chest. I glance at him. "Expecting someone?"

"No." Nate's mood darkens. He pushes himself up, gets out of bed, pulls on a pair of jeans, and pads barefoot to the door. "I'll be right back."

There's something about his eyes and the lines of his mouth that make me worry. He knows who's there, and he doesn't want to talk.

After Nate disappears through the door, he pulls it shut behind him. I'm not waiting here for someone to walk in. I jump up, tug on my clothes, and smooth my bedhead into a ponytail, before creeping toward the door. I try to listen, but I can't make out anything they're saying.

There are voices. Two men I don't know and Nate. At first, it's just the Charlie Brown's teacher muffled mumbling, but then it gets louder. I crack the door open ever so slightly and peer through the crack. Two men stand in front of Nate. One wears a uniform—maybe a cop—and the other wears a suit. They're trying to hand him a letter, but Nate won't take it.

Every muscle in Nate's back is taut like he might hit something. "This is bullshit!"

"It's the law, Mr. Smith," the uniformed man replies without raising his voice. The guy is young, Nate's age, and glances at the suit like he wishes he were somewhere else, doing something less shitty.

Nate barks back, "It can't be. This has nothing to do with me!"

"It's all explained here, Mr. Smith." The suit tries to hand Nate the envelope again, but Nate backs off like the thing could hurt him. "You realize speaking to you is sufficient for our purposes, as is leaving this in your house. I'm sorry. I realize this is a trying time for you."

"Don't pretend you give a fuck about me or what I've been dealing with. I know you don't give a shit. Just take your rent-a-cop and get out."

The officer tips his head to the side, indicating they should leave. The young man exits the house first, and only the suit remains. The guy is older with a rounded profile backlit by the setting sunbeams shining through the glass door. His jowls say he's done this before and that he didn't like doing it then either. Pity mingles with hope in his old, scarred face. His gray hair is clipped so short he might as well be bald.

"I don't know you from Adam, kid, but I'll tell you something important—fight your battles one at a time. If you try and jump into the ring with all your demons at once, you'll never make it out alive."

"Spare me the fatherly advice and get the hell out," Nate growls. From the way he's behaving, I think the old guy made a fairly accurate statement.

The suit laughs and shakes his head. "Youth is wasted on the young. You have so many choices here, but you're running blind." He glances past Nate and sees me looking through the crack in the door. I startle, but the guy doesn't give me away. He looks straight at me and says, "There are decisions to be made, and a sounding board is your best option right now.

Someone that isn't knee-deep in this shit, Nathan."

Nate glances up and softens at that, tucks his hands into the crooks of his elbows. "I didn't choose this."

"I know you didn't, but it happened all the same." The suit doesn't say another word. He slips through the door and Nate remains planted in that spot long after he's gone.

I finally creep out of the bedroom. Nate hasn't moved. He's got his feet shoulder width apart, arms folded across his chest, and his stubbled jaw locked tight. He glances over his shoulder, sees me there, and turns slowly. A plastic smile spreads across his beautiful face, marring it with pain. "I lost it, Kerry. I haven't got a fucking thing left of my past."

I don't understand. We're standing in his house, surrounded by things from his childhood. "What are you talking about?"

Nate gestures toward the envelope on the table. "He owns it and all the contents. I'm not even supposed to be here." Nate is shaking, whether from fear or anger, I don't know. He clutches the sides of his head and grits his teeth trying not to scream.

"Who? Nate, what are you talking about?"

He rounds on me, his eyes narrow and screams the words, "He owns this house and always has! It wasn't my father's house to give to me."

"Who?"

"That prick who had an affair with my mother." He says the name through gritted teeth, "Ferro."

COMING SOON:

SECRETS & LIES 5

***

Make sure you don't miss it! Text HMWARD
(one word) to 24587 to receive a text reminder
on release day.

***

Turn the page to enjoy a free excerpt of
STRIPPED 2:
A FERRO FAMILY NOVEL

CHAPTER 1: CASSIE

With Jon's coat wrapped around my shoulders and the blanket draped over my hips, I watch the two women on stage. Their laughter rings true, and I can't help feeling envious. Their lives must be so much easier than mine. I haven't laughed myself sick for a very long time. A combination of tears and terror ward off any moments of pure bliss.

I feel Jon's gaze on the side of my face. He leans close so we're nearly cheek-to-cheek and whispers, "As far as I know, they both have a bag of demonic cats living in their brains. That chick," he nods at Sidney, "confronted my mother."

My jaw drops and I stare at him, gaping. "No." The word is drawn out, and my unspoken question hangs in the air—who has the balls to challenge Constance Ferro?

"Yes. That one," he points to Avery, "she's still fighting the tide, but refuses to go under."

"How do you know that?"

He shrugs. "I sense it." I suspect there's a story behind his comments, but Jon dodges further discussion by joining Trystan by the stage.

Trystan Scott—blue-eyed heartthrob, sex on a stick, and all around ladies man—pushes back into the dark leather chair, worry pinching the tanned skin between his eyebrows. Dark hair falls into his eyes as he claws the arm of his seat, backing away from the crazy chick making herself at home in his lap.

Sidney and Avery stand arm in arm in mirrored poses, their opposite hands on their hips. Avery calls out, "Hey, little bro Ferro." She laughs and says to Sidney, "He's not very little is he?"

Sidney shakes her head and giggles. "I've heard nothing about him is little."

Peter, who had been standing quietly behind me, is suddenly across the room and marching up the steps. "Hey!"

Sidney smiles at him as he crosses the stage and wraps her arms around his waist. "Girls like to talk, and it's hard to avoid hearing rumors since people ask me way too frequently about you."

Peter's eyes turn into beach balls, and he nearly chokes. "Excuse me? Where do people ask you these things?"

She shrugs, ticking off a list on her fingers. "At the market, at school, in the ladies room." She looks over at Avery. "Do they bug you about Sean?"

"They think I'm a hooker, so I'm invisible." Avery picks at a spot of glitter on her arm. "Besides, my profession doesn't exactly make me a credible source. Who cares if Sean's call girl said he's huge?"

Everyone stops and gawks at her. Bryan stops teasing Trystan to give his full attention to Avery. "He hired you?"

Stunned faces snap to hers, but Avery's expression remains placid as if she's accepted it and moved on. In the echoing silence, a needle could drop and sound like a grenade.

Jon practically growls, "I don't know why anyone is shocked. We are talking about Sean." He seems pissed, and shoots a quick glance at me from the corner of his eye, then moves across the room to sit by Trystan.

There's a sinking feeling in the pit of my stomach. Based on the facial expressions of the people here with me, I'd guess it's contagious—we all feel it.

I keep my eyes down, but I hate that Jon said it. I hate the way no one tries to protect her. Strength on the outside is just that—outside. It doesn't keep the world from trampling your heart.

I find my voice, "She's more than that, you know." The words spill out, and once I start I can't stop. I jump up, dropping the jacket and blanket behind me. I pad toward him, standing there covered in glitter, my corset hoisting my breasts to my throat and my thong revealing my entire backside.

Jon realizes how it sounded and attempts to correct, but he's already flown that thought into a mountainside. "I know, but—"

"No little girl says, 'I want to be a stripper when I grow up.' Not one of us would sell sex if there'd been another way to survive. Every single woman who works here has the same story—fucked up life, no money, and no hope. Don't you dare damn her for it! If you do, you're damning me, too, and I refuse to accept your pity, or whatever the hell this is." I'm in his face, an inch from his nose, breathing hard. It looks like I'm going to pop out of my corset every time I breathe. Mounds of flesh swell well above the low neckline, glittering like twin disco balls.

I expect him to look at me, but he doesn't. Jon presses his lips together, letting his silence build between us while the others stare in shock. When his blue gaze lifts to meet mine, he tips his head to the side. No trace of a smile softens his lips. Nothing subdues his sharp look. "You don't know Sean. He'd show up with a corpse if it suited him."

Something inside me snaps. I straighten, laughing bitterly. "You're an asshole."

"No, I'm not. I'm just saying—"

"Shut up, man. She hears exactly what you're saying." Trystan peers around the girl in his lap, forgetting his own awkward situation for the moment. The girl sits perfectly still, but I can see her thoughts running wild behind her eyes.

Jon growls, "No, she doesn't. This isn't about any of you. It's about my brother and me." There's obviously a huge rift between Jon and Sean, but he's poking a bear with Pixy Stix. What does he think is going to happen?

"It might also be about your apparent distaste for working girls." Avery folds her arms over her chest and juts one hip to the side, glaring at him. "So, Little Ferro, spill it. Did your first hooker mistreat you? Or was it one of your strippers?"

Jon's body tenses and he sits so still he might explode. It's the moment of utter silence before a bomb detonates and blasts everything around it to bits. One of his fingers presses into the chair, and I see something flash across his face. It's raw, a wound that's still weeping.

He's quiet for a moment, swallows hard, then stands and walks into the office. The door closes soundlessly behind him. Something happened to him. I'm sure of that. Someone hurt him badly.

Apparently Avery senses it too because she slips off the edge of the stage and rushes toward me. "I'm sorry. I didn't know."

I glance at the closed door and then back to her pale face. "Neither did I. I'm not sure any of us did."

CHAPTER 2: JON

I feel like a fucking idiot walking away to hide in the office. I'm not a kid anymore. This shit shouldn't bother me, but it's always lurking—ready to rear its fuck-ugly face when I least expect it. Of course they all think I had hookers and strippers. I'm not a priest. I'm a Ferro. I live up to my reputation and then some. But that's not what made me back down. I know I don't see things accurately at times. I know my past taints my vision, clouds it, and makes me respond in the worst possible ways.

I sit down at the desk and stare at the packet of papers. I wonder if I'm reacting to Sean or my past. How can I protect Cass when I can't even deal with this?

There's a knock on my door, and before I can answer, Avery steps inside.

"Hey," she says, "I didn't mean to do that." She's standing there, her long brown hair sweeping over her shoulders and a somber expression on her face. She steps around the door, pushing it shut behind her with the heel of her foot. No shoes.

"You didn't do anything." I'm not telling her shit. She'll report back to Sean, and I don't want him involved in this. His chance to intercede is long gone.

I shuffle through the stack of papers on the desk, ignoring Sean's envelope. I'll look at it when she leaves.

"Maybe not, but it seemed like I found a sore spot and ripped it wide open."

I act like it doesn't matter. I'm not telling her shit. "I misspoke. Cassie is hurting. It was reasonable to assume I insulted all of you."

Avery stops in front of my desk, turns to a ninety-degree angle from me, and rests her denim-clad hip against it. She folds her arms loosely across her chest. "We're all hurting."

I glance up at her. Is that a hint? Is something going on with my brother? "Sean included?"

Her eyes dart to the side. She pushes off the desk and looks at a picture of the club on the wall. All the dancers are standing with the bouncers and the former owner, posing as if it were a yearbook picture. "You don't know him anymore, do you?"

"There's nothing about him that's worth knowing." I sound like a cold motherfucker, like I don't give a shit about my brother, but the tightening sensation in my chest tells me otherwise. The growing unease in my stomach, the way it twists like it's filled with shards of glass, reminds me of something I don't want to admit. I suppress it with one swift blow, forcing my emotions back down where they belong. "Maybe you don't know, so I'll tell you the drive-by version. Sean thinks I'm a piece of shit stuck to his shoe. No one willingly walks through shit, Avery. He's here to save his ass. It has nothing to do with me."

"You don't know him."

I appreciate the audacity of this woman. This is the first conversation we've had, beyond initial pleasantries, and she's picking a fight? I lean back in my chair and look at her. She's smart. I'd bet anything that she's scanning that picture for Cassie's face. It's not there. Cass always dodges pictures, probably because of her ex.

I roll my eyes and sit up quickly, reshuffling papers that don't need it. "I don't want to know him. There's nothing there worth saving, no way we'll ever be anything but blood. I don't give a shit what he does or if someone puts a bullet in his head. Actually, I've been waiting for it to happen. Between his past and the shitstorm in the press, it's only a matter of time. I wouldn't get too attached, Avery." It's a dick thing to say, but this conversation is over.

She takes the hint and heads to the door. Her hand rests on the knob for a second then she looks over her shoulder at me. "Too late. I'm already attached." She smiles sadly, watching me until I meet her eyes. "And no matter what you think, Sean cares about you. I see it in his eyes. I hear it in his voice when he talks about you. Think what you want, but take it from someone who knows what it's like to be utterly alone— Sean's here out of more than loyalty. You're more than blood to him. I'll see you around." She walks through the door without waiting for a reply.

Continue reading STRIPPED 2 now!

MORE FERRO FAMILY BOOKS

JONATHAN FERRO
~STRIPPED~
******

TRYSTAN SCOTT
~BROKEN PROMISES~
******

NICK FERRO
~THE WEDDING CONTRACT~
*****

BRYAN FERRO
~THE PROPOSITION~
*****

SEAN FERRO
~THE ARRANGEMENT~
******

PETER FERRO GRANZ
~DAMAGED~
******

MORE ROMANCE BY H.M. WARD

SCANDALOUS

SCANDALOUS 2

SECRETS

THE SECRET LIFE OF TRYSTAN SCOTT

DEMON KISSED

CHRISTMAS KISSES

SECOND CHANCES

And more.

To see a full book list, please visit:
www.HMWard.com/#!/BOOKS

CAN'T WAIT FOR *H.M. WARD'S NEXT STEAMY BOOK?*

★ ★ ★ ★ ★

Let her know by leaving stars and telling her
what you liked about
SECRETS & LIES 4
in a review!

ABOUT THE AUTHOR
H.M. WARD

New York Times bestselling author HM Ward continues to reign as the queen of independent publishing. She is swiftly approaching 13 MILLION copies sold, placing her among the literary titans. Articles pertaining to Ward's success have appeared in The New York Times, USA Today, and Forbes to name a few. This native New Yorker resides in Texas with her family, where she enjoys working on her next book.

You can interact with this bestselling author at:
Twitter: @HMWard
Facebook: AuthorHMWard
Webpage: www.hmward.com